DISNEY'S
My Very First Winnie the Pooh™

Pooh Visits
the Doctor

Written by
Kathleen W. Zoehfeld

Illustrated by
Robbin Cuddy

SCHOLASTIC INC.

New York Toronto London Auckland Sydney
Mexico City New Delhi Hong Kong Buenos Aires

First published by Disney Press, New York, NY.
This edition published by Scholastic Inc., 90 Old Sherman Turnpike, Danbury, CT 06816
by arrangement with Disney Licensed Publishing.

SCHOLASTIC and associated logos are trademarks
and/or registered trademarks of Scholastic Inc.

ISBN 0-7172-8865-X

Printed in the U.S.A.

"Christopher Robin says it's time for my *animal checkout*," said Winnie the Pooh. "He's bringing his doctor's kit to Owl's house now."

"Doctor's kit!?" cried Piglet. "Oh, p-p-poor P-Pooh, you're sick!"

"Sick!?" asked Pooh. "No—I'm fine. Though I must say I am feeling a bit rumbly in my tumbly."

"That must be it, then!" exclaimed Piglet.

"What's it?" asked Pooh.

"Your tummy—it must be sick," said Piglet.

"Is it?" asked Pooh.

"Isn't it?" asked Piglet.

"Why, yes, it must be. I think," said Pooh. His tummy jiggled and jumped.

"Oh dear," said Piglet. "Let's go together. It's so much more friendly with two."

"Step right in, Pooh Bear!" exclaimed Tigger, who had set up a desk near Owl's front door. "It'll be your turn to see Owl just as soon as Roo comes out."

"Christopher Robin, why do I need an *animal checkout*, anyway?" asked Pooh.

"Silly old bear," said Christopher Robin. "Not an *animal checkout*, an *annual checkup*. We need to make sure you are healthy and growing. And this time Owl will give you a special shot to help keep you well."

"A shot!?" cried Pooh. His tummy flopped and flipped.

"A shot!?" piped Piglet. "Oh dear!"

"It's okay," said Christopher Robin. "It will only hurt for a few seconds, and the medicine in the shot will keep you from getting mumps and measles and things like that."

"Bumps and weasels," whispered Pooh to Piglet. "How awful."

"Awfully," said Piglet.

Just then, Roo came bouncing out of Owl's house. "I just had my checkup—it was easy!" he exclaimed. "I'll have a blue one, Tigger, please."

Tigger blew up a nice blue balloon for Roo.

"Come this way, Pooh," said Rabbit, who was being the nurse.

"G-good luck," called Piglet.

Pooh stumped into Owl's house with Christopher Robin right beside him.

Owl's house felt toasty and warm, which was a very good thing, because Rabbit asked Pooh to please take off his shirt.

"Let's sit you up here on the table, my fine young bear," said Rabbit.

Rabbit wrapped a wide band around Pooh's arm.

He pumped air into the band, and it got tighter and tighter.

"How does it feel?" asked Rabbit.

"Tight," said Pooh.

"This gauge tells me your blood pressure is just right," said Rabbit.

"Now step on the scale, and we'll weigh and measure you. . . . Aha! The perfect height for a Pooh Bear of your age, but a bit stout. Still, nothing a little exercise won't cure . . . ."

"I do my stoutness exercises every morning," said Pooh.

"Excellent," said Rabbit. "Keep up the good work. If you'll excuse me now, I have a great many important things to tend to. Owl will be right in."

Christopher Robin nodded at Pooh encouragingly, as Owl entered with a flourish.

"Well, if it isn't Winnie the Pooh!" he exclaimed. "Splendid day for a checkup, isn't it? I say, how are you feeling?"

"A bit flippy-floppy in my tummy, actually," said Pooh.

"*Hmmm*," said Owl. "Let's see."

Owl felt Pooh's tummy. He felt around Pooh's neck and under his arms. "Everything seems to be right where it should be."

"Oh . . . good," giggled Pooh.

"Ah, and my otoscope is just where it should be, too—right here in my bag," said Owl.

"An *oh-do-what*?" asked Pooh.

"Nothing more than a little flashlight," said Owl. "And it will help me look in your ears . . . mm-hmm . . . your eyes . . . very good . . . your nose . . . excellent . . . and your mouth and throat. Open wide and say *ahhh*."

"*Ahhh*," said Pooh. Owl pressed Pooh's tongue gently with a tongue depressor.

"Wonderful!" exclaimed Owl.

Then Owl pulled a small rubber hammer from his bag. "Reflex-checking time!" he said grandly.

"What's a reflex?" asked Pooh.

"The tiniest tap on the knee, and you shall see," said Owl. Owl tapped Pooh's knee—and his leg gave a little kick.

"Oh, do that again," said Pooh. "That was fun." And Owl did do it again, so Pooh's other leg gave a little kick, too.

"Now, this instrument is called a stethoscope," said Owl. "It's made for listening."

"Listening to what?" asked Pooh.

"Your heartbeat," said Owl. "Would you like to hear?"

Pooh listened—*thump-bump, thump-bump, thump-bump*. It reminded him of a poem—a quiet and content poem. And it didn't bother him in the least when Owl said . . .

"Sit right here on Christopher Robin's lap. It is time for your shot."

"I know it will only hurt for a moment, and it will keep me from getting bumps and weasels," said Pooh bravely.

"That's mumps and measles, Pooh," said Owl.

"Could Piglet come in and hold my paw?" asked Pooh.

"Absolutely," said Owl.

When Owl was done, Rabbit popped back in with a bandage. "That'll feel better before you know it," he said, patting the bandage in place.

"Wow," said Piglet. "You didn't even cry!"

"An annual checkup is no problem for a brave bear like Pooh," said Christopher Robin.

I'm just that sort of bear, thought Pooh to himself as he wriggled back into his shirt.

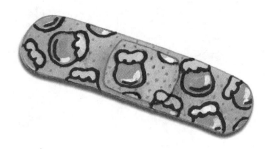

"Pooh," said Owl, "you are in tip-top shape, but that stomach of yours is a little rumbly. I prescribe a large pot of honey the moment you get home."

Pooh turned to Christopher Robin. "Press-grind a large pot . . ?" whispered Pooh. "Does that mean I can't have any more honey?"

"It means you can have a big pot of it as soon as you like," said Christopher Robin.

"I'd like it soon, then," said Pooh, whose tummy was feeling much, much better.

"T-T-F-N—ta-ta for now!" called Tigger. "Don't forget your balloon!"

"Thank you, Tigger," said Pooh. And Pooh let Piglet hold the balloon, as they stumped home together for lunch.